The Tale of Milo

Written By
Alexander Prezioso & Bethany Green

ISBN: 978-1-71694-757-5

Dedication

To all children who have ever felt different or been rejected.

From Alexander

To my wife Bree – for your compassionate heart and unwavering effort with helping children.

From Bethany

For Mia, Kelsey, Tyler & Haisley. You are all so loved.

Contents

Chapter 1
The Kingdom Awaits

O nce upon a time, on a lively farm within a desert kingdom, there lived two camels who were in love. But they were no ordinary camels. They were royalty, and the personal transportation for the King and Queen of Sulah. One day, the two camels would have a big family, and one of their camels would become the royal pet for the Princess of Sulah.

The kingdom was an extraordinary place, ruled by King Abdul and Queen Fanush. The kingdom was located in a beautiful and lush desert oasis in the Middle East. It was a gorgeous desert land with beautiful sunrises and sunsets. The oasis was filled with eucalyptus trees and wildlife seeking relief from the hot desert sands. It had farmland with a crystal-clear water spring where crops and plants flourished, and livestock went to drink.

The royal farm of the kingdom was magnificent and full of energy. It had a lot of animals that provided an abundance of food, milk, and transportation. Other than camels, the farm had Arabian horses, goats and cattle. Each type of animal had their own area to live and graze in. There was a long babbling brook that flowed in between the living areas, providing cool and crisp water for the farm animals to drink from.

The King and Queen of Sulah had a 10-year-old daughter, Princess Mia. She had beautiful long, wavy

2

excited. She began dancing around the palace singing with joy. As she was dancing, she met up with the King and Queen walking the halls of the palace.

"Oh mother, I'm so happy that I will soon have my very own camel," Mia said. She immediately ran over towards the window of the palace.

The King and Queen looked at each other and smiled. They walked slowly over to their daughter who was gazing at the farm. The Queen knelt down beside Mia, hugged her, and kissed her cheek. Mia's special day was coming.

Chapter 2

Milo

One morning, in the month of April, the mother camel gave birth to the last of her young. Her first five born were typical camels. They were tall with long legs, and had one big hump on their back. However, the last camel born was different. He was small and short, with stubby legs and two humps. The mother named this tiny camel Milo.

The mother camel was surprised to see how tiny Milo was, and that he had two humps. "Father dear, will you look at this?" the mother said.

The father camel walked towards Milo, who was

lying next to his mother. "I have never seen, in my life, a two humped camel. He is also too small," Milo's father said. Just as Milo's father turned away to tend to the other five camels, he said, "Hopefully he gets bigger."

Milo was sad to hear this from his father. He felt as if he wasn't accepted by his parents. He also felt alone as he watched his brothers and sisters playing without him. He wished one day he could walk and play with them too.

A week went by and Milo was finally able to walk around. His brothers and sisters were running around and chasing one another. Their favorite game to play was tag. Milo wanted to play too, but he could not run.

Milo walked up to his siblings while they played tag. "Hey guys! Can I play tag with you?" Milo asked.

His oldest brother, Maximus, said, "No you can't, you runt. You can't even run."

"Yes I can. Watch me," Milo said. Milo started to run, but couldn't. The faster he tried to run, the wobblier his legs got. Suddenly, Milo lost balance, and tripped over his own legs. He fell crashing into a muddy puddle.

All of his brothers and sisters started to laugh at him. They made fun of Milo, calling him 'runt,' and laughed at his second hump. "Hey Milo, you should have a cow eat one of your humps," one of his brothers yelled out to him. They all laughed louder as they walked away from Milo, leaving him in the puddle.

Milo began to cry. His entire body was wet and dirty from the mud. After a few minutes of crying, he stood up and walked over to the feeding area where his brothers and sisters were eating.

"Can you please move over so I can eat?" Milo asked. One of his sisters stopped eating, turned around and said, "No. It looks like you have plenty in that extra hump of yours." They all laughed at Milo, and tried blocking him from the feeding bin.

Milo's mother called him over to where she was eating, and moved over so that Milo could eat. As Milo ate, his mother scolded him for being dirty. "Milo, the next time you come to eat, you need to wash yourself first."

"Why does he need to do that?" one of his brothers asked. "He's ugly. He doesn't need to be clean."

Milo's parents ignored the comment and continued eating. Milo felt worse than before and lost his appetite. He slowly stepped back and walked away to wash himself over at the water spring.

After cleaning himself up, Milo went to lie down for bed. As he tried falling asleep, he looked around the farm. He thought to himself, perhaps he would try to make friends with the other animals. After a few minutes, Milo fell asleep feeling hopeful that tomorrow he would be able to make new friends and finally feel accepted.

Chapter 3

A New Idea

The next day Milo woke up feeling excited and determined to make new friends. After breakfast, his brothers and sisters went off to play tag, leaving Milo by himself. Although Milo pretended not to let it bother him, he felt sad inside because his parents ignored him, and his brothers and sisters were mean to him.

Milo looked around at the other animals on the farm. He decided first to make friends with the cattle. The cattle lived on the grassy area near the barn and water spring. It was a perfect area for them to walk around and to graze the tallest sections of the grass.

After he got enough courage, Milo walked over to the cattle area. "Will you come over and play with me?" he asked.

"Are you okay?" asked one of the cattle. The rest of them ignored Milo. "I've never seen a camel with two humps before."

"I'm okay. I was born this way," Milo said. "I can run now too. Will you play with me?"

"I'm sorry Milo but we can't. You are too small to play with us. You need to go back and play with your kind."

_ Milo slowly lowered his long neck in disappointment and walked away from the cattle. After walking for some time, not paying attention to where he was going, he looked up. He noticed a
12

group of horses further out into the grassy field, running and jumping. Milo's heart raced and he got excited. He thought it looked like a lot of fun, so he walked over to the horses.

"What are you doing?" Milo asked.

One of the younger and smaller horses galloped over to Milo and said, "We are jumping. Do you want to join us?"

"I would love to join you, but I don't know how to jump," Milo said embarrassed.

"I'll teach you. It's really easy to do and it's a lot of fun once you get the hang of it."

Milo was excited and relieved. He not only found a new friend, but was going to learn how to run and jump.

As Milo's new friend began to cover the basics in doing a run and jump, a large black stallion came galloping over to their area.

"What are you doing?" the stallion shouted at Milo. "You could get hurt. You don't belong here with us, and you need to go away."

Without saying a good-bye, the younger horse turned and galloped away from Milo towards the other horses. The stallion stood there and gave Milo a cold stare, impatiently waiting for Milo to leave. Milo lowered his head, turned around, and slowly walked away.

Milo walked toward his family's area on the farm in disappointment. He was ready to give up and call it a day. Just then, he noticed the goats doing a head-butt competition.

"5, 4, 3, 2, 1, Go!" one of the older goats counted out loudly. A pair of goats were standing on top of a stack of hay bales. They started to head-butt each other, trying to knock one another off. This intrigued Milo and he walked closer to watch the competition.

"Wow, can I try this?" Milo asked.

"Of course not. You are not a goat. You don't even have horns to head-butt," one of the other goats replied.

Just as Milo turned around to ask again if he could try, one of the goats was knocked off the hay bale and rolled into Milo. Milo was crushed from the goat's fall.

"You see Milo? You can't play because you are

going to get hurt. This is a game for goats, not

camels. Would you mind leaving us so we can get

back to practicing?" the father goat asked.

Milo stood there for a few seconds in

disappointment, before he decided to walk away. He

couldn't understand why no one wanted to play with

him or be friends with him.

While walking away, towards the camel area of the

farm, Milo's head hung even lower with a sad

expression on his face. When Milo arrived back to his

family's area of the farm he noticed his family playing

tag. As he approached them, none of his family

acknowledged his presence. He decided then not to

try anymore, to skip his dinner, and to go right to bed.

That night Milo went to bed feeling alone and

unwanted, and cried himself to sleep.

Chapter 4

Farmer's Choice

Several weeks passed and it was time for the King and Queen to view the camels to make their selection for the Princess. Traditionally, the head farmer would choose a few camels and march them up to the palace for a private viewing. The palace had a beautiful archway in front of the main entrance, which had a long red carpet. It was the perfect area to keep the royal family in the shade while they observed the camels to make their selection.

Early in the morning, on the day of the selection, the head farmer walked over to the herd of camels. When he approached the area, Milo and the other camels perked their heads up out of excitement. "Alright, the farmer is here. Everyone line up!" the father camel exclaimed.

Milo and his siblings walked towards the fence line near the entrance to the farm. The entrance was near the roadway that led towards the palace.

"Why are you lining up? You're too small and ugly to be considered," said Maximus.

Milo got angry and tried to head-butt Maximus like the goats do. Maximus stood there taking the hits, but it did not affect him. "You see, I told you. You are too small."

"Alright!" their father said. "Knock it off. Line up straight and stand tall."

The farmer made his way towards the herd. He

walked the line pointing and nodding his head,

proudly knowing that the King & Queen would have

a nice group of camels to select from. When the

farmer made his way down the lineup, he noticed

something behind the largest of the camels.

"What is that?" the farmer shouted. As he stood

there with a look of confusion and disgust on his face,

Milo slowly appeared out from behind Maximus.

"Wow, would you look at that? Two humps, and

he is a runt," one of the farmer's assistants said,

walking towards Milo.

"We can't present him to the King and Queen.

This runt is not fit for royalty," the head farmer said.

"He has an extra hump and is really ugly too."

Milo's entire family in the lineup, turned and

looked at him. They began to stare at Milo with

expressions of shame. Milo stood there, embarrassed,

not knowing how to react.

"Well, we can't have him here on this farm," said

the farmer. "After the selection is made, I'm going to

take him to the market and sell him. We don't have

any use for him here."

Milo immediately felt scared when he heard this.

He quickly ran back towards the farm, but tripped.

As he fell, a dusty cloud of dirt and sand filled the air.

Everyone laughed at Milo.

"Alright. Alright. Let's go," the famer yelled. "We

must not be late for the selection ceremony," he said

waving his arm in a forward motion towards the

palace.

After Milo stood up, he ran back to his family's living area crying as the group marched up towards the palace for the ceremony. He realized that when the farmer returned he would be taken away from his family and home.

Milo had never been outside of the farm before. But then he thought about how cruel and mean everyone on the farm was to him. He imagined that maybe it would be better out in the world, away from the farm. Perhaps he could make new friends and find someone to love and accept him for who he was, and not what he looked like.

After thinking about it for a while, Milo raised his head up and said out loud, "I am leaving. I'm going to find myself some new friends, and a new family."

22

He quickly made his way to the road and began

walking towards the desert to start his new journey.

He never once looked back at the farm.

Chapter 5
The Desert

Milo's journey wasn't like he anticipated. He was off on his own, and had to be independent. He had to find his own food, water, and place to sleep. The desert was hotter, and much lonelier than the farm. As Milo continued to march through the desert on his own, he was determined to meet new friends, and to finally be accepted.

Milo enjoyed the desert. As he traveled through it, he saw a lot of different plants. His favorite plants were cacti. He saw different sized ones. Some were tiny, and some were gigantic. All of the cacti had waxy textures with sharp spines covering them completely. He loved the beautiful sunrises and sunsets that made the sky change from blue, to purple, pink, and orange. Although he loved the desert, at times, he still felt sad and lonely.

After several weeks of roaming around the desert, Milo decided it was time to try again to meet some friends. Milo traveled west towards the direction of the palace and came upon a river. Along the river were huge boulders of rock. They were enormous and gave the impression that if you stood on top of them, you could see the world.

As Milo approached the boulders he noticed some movement in-between two of them. There were four animals that looked like goats but with long bushy tails. As he got closer, they came out to greet Milo.

"What kind of animal are you?" Milo asked.

"I'm a desert coyote. These are my brothers," one of them said. "What kind of animal are you?"

Milo replied, "I'm a camel."

"I thought camels are supposed to have one hump, not two," one coyote said. The pack began to circle around Milo.

"Well, I have two," Milo replied. "I'm from the kingdom."

"You're from the kingdom? What are you doing here?"

"I ran away," Milo said nervously. All four coyotes surrounded Milo and continued to circle around him. As they got closer, Milo noticed that they looked hungry. "Yes, I ran away to make new friends."

"Well, you're not going to make new friends here, unless you want to become our dinner," said the largest of the pack.

Milo started to turn around, eagerly looking for a way to leave. Just as he tried to walk away, three of the four coyotes jumped on top of Milo, trying to bite him. Milo spun around, trying to swing them off of his back.

The largest coyote, who stood and watched his brothers attack Milo, yelled, "He's just a lonely runt, you can take him." After a few minutes, Milo was able to shake off all three coyotes. The largest coyote grew angrier and hungrier as his three brothers backed away. Milo was frightened as the largest coyote slowly approached him, growling and snarling, showing his big white sharp teeth.

Milo looked around for a way to escape, but he saw no way out. He would have to face the coyote or be eaten. The coyote pawed at the ground while staring at Milo. He then charged at Milo for one swift attack. Just as the coyote was about to bite him, Milo head-butted him in the head and knocked him to the ground. The coyote began to cry. His brothers were scared to see their big brother knocked to the ground.

"Now back away and let me leave," said Milo as he turned and looked at the other three brothers. They slowly backed away from Milo without turning their backs on him.

All four coyotes fled to a nearby hole underneath another boulder, away from where they originally encountered Milo. Although Milo felt proud for standing up for himself, he still felt discouraged that he did not make new friends. Milo continued on with his journey along the river until nightfall, when it was time to go to sleep.

Chapter 6

Practice Makes Perfect

The following day, back at the palace, Princess Mia continued her riding lessons. Milo's older brother Maximus was the camel chosen for the Princess. A special five-foot ladder was needed to get the Princess on top of Maximus because he was so tall and his legs were so long.

"Father, look at how fast I can go!" Princess Mia exclaimed, as she rode past her father, who was sitting on the outside throne.

"Mia be careful! Maximus is still too big for you to be riding that fast," her father said with a smile.

Mia ignored her father and rode the camel even

faster. "Whoooo, hoooo!" she yelled, looking back at

her father. Just as Mia turned back around she realized

she was riding too fast and tried to slow down. She

pulled back on the reigns too hard and the camel

stopped short, causing Mia to fly off of Maximus.

The King quickly stood up from his throne and

ran across the yard to where Mia landed. She laughed

while rolling around in a thick pile of hay. The King

approached her and said with a very stern voice, "Mia,

I told you to take it easy. You are very lucky you

landed in a pile of hay. You could have broken

something."

"Oh father, I'm sorry. I was just having so much

fun and wasn't paying attention. It won't happen

again. If I take it easy, can I take him for a ride out

towards the desert?"

"I don't know Mia. I don't think you have enough experience yet to ride by yourself out in the open desert. Besides, the royal guards aren't available to take you."

Mia, with a disappointed look on her face, accepted what her father told her. She walked Maximus over to the ladder to climb back up on the saddle and continue her riding lesson.

Chapter 7
Day Trip

The next day, Mia woke up extra early. She snuck out her palace window and made her way down to the farm. She quietly opened the gate to the farm, and walked straight to the camel area. She took the ladder out and set it up. Mia walked Maximus over to the ladder and climbed up on top of him.

"Ok buddy. Here we go, onward to the desert." Mia grabbed the reigns and pulled them in firmly towards her.

Mia rode past the gates of the farm and into the desert. She was fascinated with how beautiful and open the desert was. As she got further away from the farm, she rode faster.

After a few hours of riding, Mia felt worried. She was lost, and didn't know how to get back to the palace or the farm. Mia stopped riding and looked around. In the distance, she saw a white object that looked like the palace. Mia took her canteen out and took a cool drink of water. She wiped the sweat off of her face before continuing to ride.

As she traveled towards the white object in the distance, Mia looked up at the sun to see what time it was. She thought about how angry her father would be if he found out she left on her own. Maybe her father wouldn't notice that she was gone if she hurried up and got home quickly.

Mia yanked on the reigns to make Maximus go faster. She never rode this fast before, but felt good knowing that she was making progress. As Mia got closer to the white object, it started to disappear. It was a mirage! Mia looked around nervously trying to determine where she was. As she turned her head back too far, Mia lost her balance and went flying off of Maximus. A sharp pain shot up Mia's leg when she landed hard on the ground.

Mia screamed and began crying as she realized that she had broken her leg. After lying there a few minutes, she calmed herself down and got enough energy to pull herself up. Mia hobbled over to Maximus and tried to get back in her saddle, but she couldn't - he was too tall. Mia fell back down and laid in the hot sand. She yelled for help, but no one was around. She desperately looked around, but eventually passed out from the desert heat.

Maximus stood over Mia providing her shade to keep her cool. He didn't know what to do. He looked around and there was nothing in sight, and no one to help them.

Chapter 8
The River

As night fell, Milo continued to follow the river. He saw that he was making his way back towards the palace. When he realized this, he changed his course and headed back out into the desert. He remembered what it was like back on the farm, and did not want to return there.

After changing his course and walking for an hour, Milo noticed a large brown hump out in the distance. It looked similar to the boulders the coyotes lived under. He stopped and tried to look at it more closely, but then realized it was moving around – it wasn't a boulder.

As Milo got closer to the boulder shaped object, he realized it was a camel. He heard it shout "Milo, is that you?" Milo ran towards the camel. As he got closer, he realized it was Maximus.

"Milo, I need help," his brother pleaded. "The Princess fell off of me, broke her leg and is passed out. She hasn't woken up since yesterday."

"We need to get some water for her. Wait here, and I'll go get some from the river," Milo said. Milo immediately took off running. His brother felt relieved that someone else was there to help.

Thirty minutes later, Milo returned with a mouthful of cold water from the river. He walked up to the Princess and opened his mouth, dropping the cold water over her. The Princess awoke and screamed in shock from the temperature of the water.

Mia looked up and saw Milo standing over her.

She immediately noticed how much smaller Milo was,

compared to Maximus. She realized that Milo was her

only hope to ride back to the palace.

Mia grabbed on to Milo's leg and pulled herself up

about halfway. Milo lowered his neck and Mia was

able to pull herself up to a standing position.

"You are a small camel, but just the right size for

me." Mia hobbled up on top of Milo to rest perfectly

between his two humps.

"Ready to lead the way?" Milo asked Maximus.

"I don't know how to get back. I'm lost. She had

me riding around in circles for hours. I'm so tired."

"It's okay, I know the way. We'll head back

towards the river and follow it to the farm, then to the palace," Milo said proudly.

After a few hours of traveling, they came up to the river. There was a set of boulders there, and out from underneath them came the coyotes. They could smell the blood from Mia's broken leg. This time, the pack had six coyotes. The coyotes quickly ran up to Mia, Milo and Maximus. They circled around them. They stared at Mia. She looked back at them extremely frightened, not knowing what to do. Milo's brother was scared stiff. Even though Maximus was huge compared to Milo and the coyotes, his heart raced in fear.

"I'm going to fight them off," Milo said, as he turned to look over at Maximus, who was frightened.

40

"You're going to do what? Are you crazy? They will eat you."

"The only thing that matters is the safety of the Princess. I fought them off before, and I can do it again!" Milo said. "I need to put the Princess down, and you need to guard her."

Milo quickly laid down to let the Princess slide off of him. Maximus then quickly stood over Princess to protect her. Milo stood back up and approached the coyotes.

"This time we're not going to let you win!" one of the coyotes yelled. The entire pack charged at Milo. Milo ran in circles dodging each of the attacks. He swung his neck from side to side hitting the coyotes, knocking them back on to the ground. The largest coyote got behind Milo and bit his leg. Milo fell to the ground in pain.

"You little runt. You're not going to get in the way of us getting our dinner." The coyote turned away from Milo and made his way towards the Princess. As the coyote approached the Princess, he stopped and pawed at the ground, preparing for his final attack.

Milo stood up and yelled, "Don't you call me runt!" He charged at the coyote contacting him with full force. The coyote flew up into the air over Maximus and landed hard on the ground. The coyote passed out from the blow. When the other coyotes saw this, they stood up and ran off, leaving the largest of the pack behind.

Once the coyotes were out of sight, Maximus

asked Milo where he went the day he left the farm.

Milo told him the story of how he went exploring

through the desert to make new friends and to feel

accepted. He also talked about how sad he was

because of the way he was treated back at the farm.

After Maximus heard Milo's story, he approached

Milo with regret and said, "Milo, I want to say that

I'm sorry for calling you names and treating you

differently. I was wrong. I hope that you can forgive

me. I am honored to call you my brother."

Milo walked up to his brother and stared at him

for a moment without expression, then said, "I

forgive you Maximus. Let's get the Princess home."

Milo laid back down on the ground to let the Princess

get back on top of him. As Milo stood up, Mia

reached forward and gave Milo a big hug and said, "I love you Milo. You are my hero!" The three of them resumed their travels safely back to the palace.

Epilogue

Following the weeks of Princess Mia's safe return and recovery, a special event was held at the palace. Milo was honored by the King & Queen, and was designated as the lead camel for the Princess. He also became an official member of the royal family, and was crowned.

Milo's family learned of his outstanding courage and heroism for saving both the Princess and Maximus in the face of danger. They all apologized for the way they treated him and told him how much they were proud of him.

On Milo's days off from his palace duties, he likes to play tag with his brothers and sisters on the farm.

His favorite trick while playing tag is to head-butt his brothers and sisters into the muddy puddles. On occasion, Milo joins the goats for head-butting competitions, or the horses for jumping.

Milo's favorite thing of all is to go riding with Princess Mia out in the desert. They became the best of friends and do all sorts of fun activities together. Milo finally found what he had been waiting for: love and acceptance.

Afterword

No matter how different people are, always treat them with dignity and respect. Throughout the story, Milo was treated unfairly and cruelly. However, he had an enormous amount of courage and the ability to handle stressful situations. Milo may have been different, but his unique physical characteristics allowed him to do things that others could not do. We all have abilities and differences that make us unique individuals. It is okay to be different, and it is okay for others to be different. We all have an inner beauty that needs to be discovered - it is what makes us all special. The most important things you can do are: <u>love and accept one another</u>.